# *wood* LESSONS

## HALLIE BENNETT

# BOOKS BY THIS AUTHOR

# CHAPTER ONE

*ANNA*

The empty wall mocks me as I sit on the carpet of my new apartment. A cream couch with matching coffee table surrounds me along with the rest of my unpacked bookshelves and knick knacks, but this wall stands bare except for an inset fireplace—no mantel to interrupt the flat surface.

My eyes travel over the three cube shelves I built myself, and dread at having to buy more weighs on me. After moving from the small town I'd lived in since college, I wanted to feel like an adult—someone who's actually put together. Building furniture from a box like a college kid felt like a step back from that goal.

"You're being ridiculous," I admonish myself. *Furniture doesn't make you an adult; no matter what HGTV shows.*

But I can't ignore the vision in my head of a welcoming home designed with purpose instead of a hodgepodge of things. Can't stop the dream of inviting friends over and feeling pride instead of embarrassment at the state of my home.

*What friends?*

"It'll happen," I say aloud, praying that voicing the hope will make it a reality. I promised myself with this move I'd step out of my comfort zone and be more outgoing. Part of the rut I found myself in back home was limiting my world to work and home, so socializing became harder the longer between visits with friends became. Everyone I knew lived an hour or more away with busy lives filled with husbands and children.

Somehow, I became the hermit friend despite my best intentions.

*Not this time.*

Crawling over to the laptop resting on the coffee table, I start searching for small businesses that specialize in custom furniture—a clear image of a beautiful mantel and bookcase becoming the focal point of the room appearing in my mind's eye.

The vision symbolized friendship and community. A piece of furniture tangled with my dream—two seemingly unrelated things symbolizing the bright future I hoped to build.

Releasing a deep breath, I shrug. "Here goes nothing."

TWO WEEKS AND MULTIPLE email exchanges later, I turn onto a gravel drive, following it to the home of CC Designs. Their reviews mentioned excellent service with quick turnaround times, so I'd messaged them for a quote. Spending so much money made me uneasy, but I figured it meant quality. Besides, could I really put a price on my dream of hosting friends? Something this piece was a key part of?

Reassuring myself, I keep driving until a large barn set back from a house looms ahead. Today, I'm inspecting the progress made, and nerves cause sweat to gather under my arms.

These are professionals while I'm just a woman pretending to know what I'm doing. Imposter syndrome rides me hard, but fake it until you make it, right? Normal people do this all the time which means I can handle it, too.

Parking next to a black SUV, I breathe deeply in an effort to calm my racing heart before grabbing my purse and getting out. Despite being fifteen minutes from the city limits, the area looks like it belongs on a mountainside with forests of trees surrounding it. Wind ruffles the treetops, carrying the whine of power tools emitting from the barn.

A woman steps outside of the house and waves. "Hi! You must be Anna; I'm Cora. Did you have any trouble finding us?"

I shake my head and force a confident smile. "Nope; for once GPS didn't lead me astray." Plus, I'd driven by their entrance earlier to double-check the address, but she didn't need to know about my paranoid behavior.

Cora laughs then continues, "Awesome! Peter and Chris are in the barn working on some projects right now. I can show you what we have done so far, and you can see part of the process. Sound good?"

Nodding in agreement, we begin walking towards the barn, our shoes crunching the gravel underneath.

"So, this is your first custom piece?"

"Yep, I felt very adult going over all the details." I joke, thankful for the brief easing of tension coalesced in my neck and shoulders.

"Ha! I still feel that way, and we've been doing this for four years now."

"When does it stop being adulting and start being just living? Maybe when we're like fifty?" A running gag between my friend group flickers in my mind. We used to laugh about how close we were to forty in college like that number meant something important, and now the age keeps shifting as we grow older.

She shakes her head, sending the high ponytail swishing back and forth. "Maybe..."

We reach open barn doors where I can see one guy using a power saw while another looks to be marking a two by four.

"Hey!" I jump at Cora's unexpected shout. One man looks up then taps the other who turns off the saw and removes his safety glasses. *Damn, these are some good looking men.* They both have plain tees under open plaid shirts with dark jeans and boots—exactly what I'd imagine a guy who works with his hands to wear.

"Guys, this is Anna. She ordered the bookcase mantel. Anna, this is Peter and my husband, Chris." She gestures to the blonde who bows his head in greeting.

Peter comes over to shake my hand. "Nice to meet you."

A blush stains my cheeks as I return the sentiment. His rough hand sends my imagination into overdrive as it leaps to past fantasies of lonely lumberjacks claiming their women.

*You've just met the man; no one's claiming you.*

"She's here to see the progress we've made. Join us, you're the one doing the bulk of the building on this one," Cora says.

Shoving the ridiculous thoughts aside, I take a deep breath and remind myself I'm here on business, not to drool over this attractive man. *Save that for later.*

When we reach my project, a plea runs through my mind: *please don't embarrass yourself by asking stupid questions.*

"So, what do you think?"

Even unfinished, it's beautiful—the perfect statement piece. Relief that I made the right decision relaxes my tense muscles. "Wow, it's amazing." I reach forward to touch it when Peter quickly grabs my hand.

"Careful; it's not completely sanded yet." His gruff voice softens as I freeze at the contact.

"Sorry." My hand pulls back, but it takes a second for him to let go. *Or you wish he hesitated*, I berate myself. *Pull yourself together. Remember: professional.*

"Right..." Cora glances at Peter before returning to me. "You can see that the base is built, and once Peter's done sanding, I'll get started with priming and painting. But you're satisfied with the work so far?"

"Definitely; it's way better than I imagined." Massive, towering over my short stature, I'm grateful I won't be the one carrying it up my apartment stairs.

"Did you want to add anything else like doors? Because now would be the time to do it," Cora asks, making notes on her phone.

"No, I think this is fine." I'd already gone back and forth with the door idea and didn't want to revisit the debate.

"In that case, I think we're good here, Peter. Anna and I will finish up with the color choices. Thanks for your help!"

Peter nods, his gaze lingering on mine before leaving with us following behind to head towards the house. Cora's studio is in the front room, shining bright with creams and blues decorating the walls and furniture. It resembles one of the HGTV showrooms I'd thought of when I came up with this original plan.

After an hour talking about different shades of grey, which I oddly enjoy as a graphic designer, we finish and go back outside where the guys are taking a break. Both of them rest against a wooden bench with water bottles held between their hands.

"All done?" Chris asks as we reach them while Peter straightens to his full height—the gesture of respect warms me. Maybe chivalry isn't dead, after all.

"Yep! How are things here?"

"Good, we've made a decent headway on the Garth family's collection." He gestures to a table and two chairs with intricate legs sitting at the edge of the barn's concrete floor.

Admiration washes through me, and I absentmindedly murmur, "I wish I could do stuff like that."

"I could teach you," Peter suggests, confounding me with the immediate offer. Chris and Cora exchange confused looks while I struggle to decide if he's being serious.

"Oh, no, That's not—"

He cuts me off in a rush. "I have everything at my shop, and once you have the tools it's easy to get started. We could make a simple birdhouse for you to try first. Very basic." Earnest grey eyes bore into me, and my potential answer hangs in the air like it's of vast importance to him.

*Yes or no. What's it gonna be?*

"Alright, sure. I'd like that," I agree.

Why not? I want to change my life, right? Old me would never agree to spending time alone with a man I don't know—especially not a man as hot as Peter. Anxiety about sounding dumb or humiliating myself would be too much of a risk to take.

*Who are you kidding?*

I'll still be nervous, but I'm committed now.

"Cool, I can get your number from Cora, and we can work something out."

"Sounds good," I say, speculating if this is his smooth way of getting my number or if he's genuinely being a nice guy offering lessons. *Probably the latter.*

"Yeah..." Cora drawls as she stares at Peter who avoids her scrutiny, mumbling something about getting back to work and waving good-bye. Taking my cue, I drag my focus away from his retreating form, excuse myself, and head home—the drive flying by in a haze as I replay the afternoon.

# CHAPTER TWO

### PETER

"What was that about?" Cora corners me before I start sawing through another plank.

"What?" I play dumb, knowing what she's asking but unwilling to answer. Hell, a logical response escapes me because I don't know why I offered to teach Anna. It's not something I've done before. Usually, I don't say much at all when clients come by. That's Cora's job.

But the moment I saw Anna step into the shop, she drew me in like a moth to flames, and instinctively, I'd pitched the idea.

"Come on; teaching her how to woodwork? Since when do we offer that service?" She crosses arms over her chest and waits for an explanation.

"It's not like that; I'm not gonna charge her or anything." I just want to spend time with her, but Cora doesn't need that information.

"Oh, really?" Cora raises her eyebrows. "Do you have a crush, Peter?"

I ignore the ridiculous question, tightening my grip on the hand saw.

"You're blushing! Oh my god, you do!" She pokes my side and laughs. "Good thing we don't have a no fraternization policy."

I scoff at her needling. "It's just woodworking; chill out. You're getting way ahead of yourself."

"Mhmm...But you guys would be a cute couple—the curvy brunette with the tall carpenter. I can see it now."

"Cora, you're my boss, so you'll understand when I say if you want this set finished on time, you need to leave me alone. Go bug your husband, instead." With that, I shove safety glasses and protective ear muffs on and start the saw, drowning out any objections she may have.

The peace of building things with my hands and getting lost in the work calms my rapid heartbeat. It's comforting living in the dulled world—the buzz of the saw cocooning me.

Always has, always will.

But it doesn't prevent the loneliness waiting to creep in at night. Sometimes, it's so strong I end up back in the garage working on projects until my eyes refuse to stay open any longer—a danger when dealing with sharp blades.

Carving and whittling used to be enough to stave off the unpleasant emotion, but lately they've lost their effectiveness. Having someone to share life with would help; too bad single women don't frequent my house or the CC Designs studio that often.

*Until today...*

But it's more than availability, I realize, shooting down the assumption that the attraction I feel would be the same for any woman who appeared. A few have visited out here—not many, but some—and I never had this reaction to any of them.

It's all Anna.

A vulnerability in her eyes that beckons me, and a shyness I recognize in myself, making me curious to see if we could overcome it together. *That's a lot of pressure, man.*

Wiping my sleeve across the sweat on my brow, I overlook the warning in my head and choose to focus on the possibility of Anna...and a future filled with love instead of emptiness.

MY PHONE RINGS THREE days later as I amble back to the cabin after double-checking everything is set for Anna when she arrives this afternoon. Looking down, her name appears on the screen and my throat tightens. "Hey, Anna, what's up?"

For a second, I wonder if she's about to cancel our first lesson, fear making it difficult to swallow. We've texted to arrange this time, but it hasn't gone past a professional tone—no matter the multitude of questions threatening to burst from me.

"Well, I think I might be lost. I've been up and down this road, my GPS says I'm here, but I don't see anything." Music lowers while the phrase "You have arrived at your destination" repeats in the background.

"Are you on Racine? Because the turn off for my drive is right after you round the curve over the creek." Miles outside of town, winding roads are common around here, and it's easy to miss hidden drives with the dense trees lining the area.

"Alright, I think I know what you're talking about, let me—" The phone muffles her voice when I hear a scream, and the line goes dead.

"Anna? Anna!" Panic spikes in my blood at the sudden silence. Accidents occur at that bend all the time due to people not slowing down when taking it, and worry slices through me that Anna could be hurt. Racing to my truck, I barrel down the drive, kicking up a cloud of dust. Time slows like molasses despite my lead foot on the gas.

*Please be okay...*

Finally, I round the curve to see Anna's car pulled off to the side; it doesn't look like it's dented from hitting a deer or anything which allows my grip on the steering wheel to loosen. When I make a U-turn to park behind the vehicle, she comes into view, peering down at the creek from the top of a ditch.

"Thank God." I exhale a ragged breath and hurry to check on her. "Are you alright?"

She jerks at the sound of my voice and slips in the slick grass with a yelp. Before I can reach her, she slides down into the muddy creek below.

"Fuck! Anna, are you okay?" I carefully make my way down until my pants and shoes are soaked from standing in a foot of water.

"Yeah, I'm fine; you scared me, though. I wasn't expecting anyone to be out here."

"Sorry," I apologize, bending to provide stability as she tries to stand. "When I heard you scream on the phone I was worried something had happened, so I drove down here to check on you."

Her drenched clothing clings to bountiful curves, giving me a delightful show of hills and valleys I long to touch—uncaring of the mud streaks marring the outfit.

*Not the time.*

Steering my gaze upwards, I ask, "What happened?"

Red spreads from her chest to her cheeks as she ducks her head. "Um...a family of ducks were crossing the road. I slammed on my brakes, so I wouldn't hit them. That's why I'm down here—watching them swim away."

*Damn, could she be more adorable?*

"I'm glad they crossed safely, but we should get you clean. That mud will dry soon which won't be a pleasant experience."

Anna nods in agreement, and we trudge up the bank with me sticking close in case she loses balance. "Wait here, and I'll grab something from my truck to protect your seat. Then you can just follow me."

"I don't want to inconvenience you." She brushes a hand over cheek, leaving a smear of dirt. "I'll go home, and we can reschedule for another time."

"Nonsense. My home's a few minutes away; that beats driving home in the state you're in."

*And I don't want you to go.*

An irrational fear that she won't return forms a knot in my stomach. I need her to stay, to be given a chance—prove I'm worth the trouble of coming out here.

My mind conjures one way to keep her interested: me scrubbing her naked body clean before fucking her against the shower wall.

*Because an orgasm guarantees commitment? Get real, buddy.*

"If you're sure..." Her hesitant voice reminds me we're nowhere near that stage yet; I still need to convince her to come home with me.

"I am. Trust me; it's not a problem. Just hang on, and I'll be right back." Jogging to my truck, I snag a blanket kept in the cab for emergencies and present it with a flourish. "It's not pretty, but it'll do the job."

A cautious smile tugs at her mouth, and I accept it as a good sign. Anna takes the offering and spreads it over her front seat. Once she's settled, it's not long before we merge onto the road towards my cabin, and soon I'm leading her to the master bathroom in my bedroom—skipping the usual house tour.

"Take your time." I gesture to the large shower, tamping down the yearning to touch her. "I'll lay out some clothes for you to change into when you're finished."

Uncertainty shines in her eyes. "Thank you, but are you sure you don't want to go first?" Her hands wave at my muddy pant legs.

*I'd rather we conserve water and shower together.*

But the suggestion stalls on my tongue. "Positive. I'll wipe down with a rag in the spare bathroom.

"Okay... I won't be long." Her shy smile makes me lightheaded with desire, my cock swelling behind the zipper of my jeans. Forcing a calm outward demeanor, I leave Anna alone to wash up, counting my steps in an attempt to have anything besides her soapy, naked body filling my thoughts.

After replacing my soiled jeans, my stomach growls, and food seems like a good option since lunchtime is nearing.

*Plus, it'll keep her here longer.*

I don't know what's come over me, but it's like every dormant caveman instinct I have is making itself known. Seeing to her needs is my top priority, and they tick off one by one in my head. First, get her clean. Then, feed her. And finally, fuck her until she's so satisfied, she'll never want to leave.

A rueful chuckle escapes at that last part because it's not going to happen today. Opening the fridge, cool air chills my skin. Pulling out the ingredients for sandwiches, I hope Anna likes turkey. Red tomato slices join a platter piled with lettuce leaves while I move on to cutting an avocado apart.

The soft pattering of feet notifies me of Anna's arrival before I see her appear around the corner. Curling wet strands frame her face while crossed arms cause my tee to stretch over her abundant breasts—pushing them tight against the cotton.

"How are you feeling?" Swallowing hard, I center my attention on avoiding blood loss as I finish slicing the avocado.

"Better, thank you." She moves closer and takes a seat at one of the barstools behind the island I'm working at. Looking around the combined space of my kitchen and living room, she continues, "You have a beautiful home. Did you make any of the pieces here?"

My chin lifts in pride at her praise. Good to know the years spent renovating and building my own furniture had paid off. "Yes, I built all of the woodwork: tables, bookshelves. For a while, it looked pretty bare in here."

"That's really impressive; I wish I had such a useful skill." She sighs and leans her head on a propped fist. An aura of wistfulness radiates from her.

"Well, that's what I'm going to help you with, right? And don't be so hard on yourself; I'm sure you have a lot of talents." I set a plate in front of her with the sandwich, avocado slices, and some chips I found in the cabinet.

"Thank you for doing this." She motions to the food before taking a bite. A low hum of approval vibrates from her and straight to my groin. What I wouldn't give to hear her make that sound with my cock down her throat.

*Down, boy.*

"I suppose I'm good at graphic design. But that doesn't really translate to tangible, useful things, you know? Printing a design and hanging it on a wall isn't the same as building a table for people to gather around," she explains as a glimmer of sadness enters her brown eyes. The reasoning reveals insight into a piece of Anna. My work helps build community while hers is a singular creation—at least in her mind.

"Great design brings people together, too. Groups gather around priceless art all the time. Don't cut yourself short." The corner of her mouth lifts up in a half-hearted smile as if she doesn't believe me but appreciates the effort.

"You've got a point. And I am trying to get into more website design which benefits a lot of people. It just doesn't feel on the same level as your work, though there's really no comparison." Her eyes glance upward in exasperation. "Sorry, I'm rambling, and I doubt I'm making much sense. Ignore me."

"No, I get it. You don't need to apologize." My determination to help her solidifies. I'd already planned on teaching her, but it was mostly a ruse to be near her. Now, I understand it means more to her than a random hobby.

After that, we eat in a contemplative silence until our plates are cleared—uncertain of what to do now.

"Well, I should probably get going..." She trails off, tucking an errant curl behind her ear. I circle the island unsure of my next move when she hops off the barstool and trips over the dragging hem of my oversized sweatpants. "Oh!"

Anna falls forward into my arms—exactly where I want her. Embarrassment is plain on her pink cheeks while her nails dig into my arms for balance. Seeing my opportunity, I bend down and press my mouth to hers.

Soft lips part in astonishment, and I surge deeper—tongue sweeping across hers, sending a moan of pleasure through us both at the contact. This is what I've been waiting for since the moment I saw her at Cora's. To touch and taste her. My hands cup Anna's round hips and urge her closer, heat burning through our layers of clothes.

*Fuck, she's sweet, and I'm hers: hook, line, and sinker.*

# CHAPTER THREE

*ANNA*

Peter's bruising grip should scare me. This kiss should scare me. Yet, fear isn't the dominant emotion running through my veins—wild excitement is.

This afternoon hasn't gone at all like I expected from the wayward ducks on the road, to showering in Peter's home, and now his teeth nibbling at my lips. Maybe I should be more careful about what I wish for because I'm not sure how many life-altering events I can handle.

Though, as far as first kisses go, this is better than I expected.

"Sorry, I couldn't resist," Peter whispers as we separate, but he doesn't release me. "You're so goddamn pretty."

The compliment warms me from the inside out; usually people comment on my intelligence or how reliable I am—never anything physical. The logical, feminist part of me thinks that's how it should be, but as a woman, it's nice to hear that I'm attractive, too.

A nervous chuckle escapes as I search for something to say before settling on the obvious. "Um, thank you..."

"But you didn't like it?" He guesses as my sentence fades.

"No, I did! It's just..." I lift my hands helplessly, confused. "How do people usually respond after a kiss?"

"You don't know?" Curiosity instead of judgment coats his tone, but my brain still scrambles for a way to brush the question off. It's not something I like to share—that I've never been kissed.

Throughout high school I assumed it would eventually happen, then I graduated and pinned my hopes on college. Neither panned out, and as I slowly became a hermit, any chance of my kissing status changing floated further and further away.

Silence lingers between us, turning awkward. Dropping my hold on his arms, I attempt to put space between us—to form an invisible layer of protection around myself—but Peter refuses to let go. Resigned, I decide to take the plunge and lay my cards on the table.

"This was my first kiss."

His hands flex on my waist, and I catch a glimpse of kindness in his eyes. "Why's that, baby?"

"I'm not the most outgoing person; it's difficult for me to make friends. Not the greatest dynamic for guys wanting to know me—let alone, kiss me." My jaw clenches at the explanation; I hate admitting to failing at something everyone else seems to have mastered.

"It's not your fault—being shy isn't an excuse for a man to ignore you. In my mind, it just means I need to work harder to make you feel comfortable enough to trust me with your thoughts and feelings."

The earnest sentiment sends butterflies fluttering around my stomach; his sincerity leaves no doubt that he means it. "Well, you're the exception, though I'm not sure how much I made you work before our kiss."

"To be fair, you tumbled into my arms without much warning. How could I resist the temptation?" He grins, revealing the small gap between his teeth.

*Many men have...* My insecurity pipes up.

"If we're being honest, you're *my* exception." The assertion startles me, and I study his serious expression. "My life consists of work and home; I don't really get out much. But when I saw you..."

He runs a hand through his hair, ruffling the short layers. "Something clicked, and I found myself offering these lessons before I could even think through why."

The fact that my presence compelled him to break his usual routine boosts my ego—especially in light of my own recent confession. This man has all the right words, but is he too good to be true?

"Looks like we're both stepping out of our comfort zones."

"Guess so." We share a look of understanding, a fragile bond of intimacy weaving between us. And optimism sprouts as I consider the possibilities of our growing friendship.

LATER, I FIND MYSELF in a crowded bar with my co-worker, Jess. Double-booking my schedule with two separate meet-ups pleased me even as social fatigue began to cloud my brain.

*Don't complain; this is what you wanted.*

A social life meant hanging out with people when they were available—even if it was nearing my bedtime. Off-key singing belts from the stage towards the back of the bar as Karaoke Night commences. I don't plan on signing up but supporting Jess is doable. Maybe one day all of my baby steps will lead me to taking the stage; however, tonight I'd settle for cheering from my seat.

"So, how was your thing today? Didn't you say you were meeting some guy about wood lessons? What does that even mean?" Jess downs a shot of tequila and grabs another while I sip my cocktail. She's fielding a ton of free drinks from men, and I'm a little impressed by her haul.

"He's teaching me the basics of building chairs, tables, and whatever."

Her nose scrunches while a short laugh bursts out. "And why do you need to learn these skills? Planning a career change?"

I laugh and shake my head, dislodging a curl from my bobby pins. "No, I just thought it'd be a fun opportunity to try something new."

"Hmm... And what about this Peter? Is he hot?" The music cuts out as the song ends, so her shouted words draw attention to us. I want to sink into the sticky floor as prying eyes focus on our conversation.

Keeping my voice low and even, I lean forward. "Yes, he is, but that's not why I agreed to the sessions."

*Liar.*

"Oh, tell me more. Do you have a picture?" Jess's excitement is catching, and the tiredness I felt earlier starts to fade at the ability to divulge my feelings and gossip about the man in my life.

*He's not officially your man, though, is he?*

But he's close enough if our kiss counts for anything, and I'm not above milking it. With friends back home dating and getting married, usually, I'm on the other end of these conversations. The switch in roles feels good.

"Of course not! It would've been weird to snap a photo, but he's tall and..." The rest of the night passes with Jess gushing over my good fortune while I bask in the praise. Peter may not be my boyfriend—he may not want more than a short fling, if that—but I'd enjoy this fluttery emotion of a crush until we say our final farewell.

# CHAPTER FOUR

*PETER*

The beeping of the microwave echoes in the kitchen, and I remove the heated dinner of turkey and mashed potatoes. Red and orange light spills onto the linoleum as the sun sets, marking another day ending with me alone in my cabin.

Sitting at the square top kitchen table, my eyes avoid the three empty chairs around me. *It won't always be like this.* The refrain provides little comfort, though.

Every night is the same, and I wish Anna were here. We've texted since our kiss—conversations that brightened my day every time a message came through. And I could use some brightening right about now.

Tossing my fork on the empty plate, I sit back with a groan and play with the idea of calling her. Would it be too desperate? My foot taps a frenzied beat on the hardwood floor as I contemplate the decision.

*Screw it.*

Unlocking my phone, I scroll to Anna's number before hitting the call button. Food churns in my stomach at the dull ringing as I wait for her to answer like a schoolboy after sending his crush a valentine.

"Hello?"

"Hey, it's Peter. Sorry to bother you; I just thought it'd be nice to talk," I say stupidly, my lack of a plan obvious. "I'm not interrupting anything, am I?"

"Nothing but my Netflix binging; this is probably a better use of my time." A short laugh muffles over the line, and my jaw unclenches at the welcome sound.

*This was the right choice.*

"So, how did your pitch go?"

"I'm amazed you remember..." Bewilderment laces her tone.

*Baby, I remember everything you say.*

"It went well, I think. They thanked me for my time but didn't say much else. Honestly, I was relieved to get it over with; I was a sweaty, nervous wreck."

"You don't have anything to worry about. I saw the design; you did a great job." She'd sent me a couple pictures of the website she'd created for a new client at her company the other day. From what I could tell, the minimalistic design fit the brief she'd described perfectly.

"I appreciate the boost of confidence, but we don't know what the other pitches looked like. There are a lot of talented people at the firm. I'm still relatively inexperienced." A crackling rattles in my ear like she's opening a package, and I picture her making dinner in the galley kitchen she'd described in an earlier conversation.

"Don't sell yourself short, babe." Walking to the living room, I relax into the couch, prepared for an evening of talking with my girl—the loneliness I'd been feeling melting away.

SATURDAY DAWNS COOL and cloudy. Anna's rescheduled lesson is today, and I can't wait to see her. I considered asking if she wanted to meet beforehand for a date but figured it might be safer sticking to the plan. Not to mention, the off-chance of her rejection scares me.

Rolling out of bed, I take a quick shower and grab a protein bar for breakfast before heading outside. Everything's ready for her visit after I spent the night organizing the shop.

The familiar task reminded me of her last visit—rife with hiccups. Hopefully, we can avoid any mishaps this time around. Though, I wouldn't mind kissing her again.

Numerous unfinished projects line the shelves in my garage. Choosing one of my hobby projects, I kill time by working on the small birdhouse. The trees out back are full of these, swarms of birds calling them home—something I imagine Anna loving considering her episode with the ducks.

Pop music drifts in the air along with the hum of an engine. Setting the piece back on the shelf, I wipe my hands on a rag before going to welcome Anna with an impromptu hug. She stiffens at the contact, and I worry that I've misinterpreted our exchanges.

"Hey!" She finally returns the gesture, wrapping her arms around my waist.

*Relax, man. Don't overthink everything.*

"Glad to see you made it okay on the second try." I quip as I reluctantly drop my hold, and we start walking towards the workshop beside my cabin.

"Well, the directions are burned in my memory after the last debacle." Amusement twinkles in her eyes. "Though, those ducks were pretty cute."

"Hmm, I know someone else who fits that description."

*Cheesy, fucker.... Don't care.*

# CHAPTER FIVE

## ANNA

The remark warms me, no matter how corny. It eases my anxiety to know his flirting is on par with mine—almost nonexistent. But the sweet attempt is appreciated.

Sawdust floats in the weak sunlight as we step inside the detached garage for my first lesson. The dust tickles my nose, though the scent of freshly-cut wood is comforting.

"It's not much compared to Cora and Chris's barn, but it works for my side projects," Peter explains as he waves an encompassing hand towards the arrangement of tools and tables. One large rectangular table dominates the center of the garage with a table saw resting at one end; counters of various hand tools and projects line the walls.

"Do you make a lot of those? And sell them?" I ask, curious since his cabin is already outfitted with handmade pieces of furniture.

"Sometimes. When someone approaches me for a personal project and time allows me to work on them." He shrugs, making the plaid tighten around his broad shoulders. "But I don't really seek it out; it's not like I have a website or anything. It's all word of mouth through my work with CC Designs."

"It's impressive, however you get business. Means people really admire your work. Are you thinking of going solo?" My hand traces the smooth edges of an unfinished chair propped to the right of me. Intricate lines wrap around the legs, probably taking long hours to create such a detailed design. And it occurs to me that he's as much of an artist as I am—just in a different field.

"Not particularly. I'd actually prefer becoming partners with Chris and Cora."

"What do they think of that plan?"

A rueful chuckle echoes in the garage. "Not sure. I haven't asked them yet. Still a little hesitant about making the leap."

His reluctance baffles me, though I relate to his fear. Peter's clearly talented; I wouldn't assume he'd be afraid to approach them. "I felt the same way before moving here. I felt it so much that I put off making a final decision for more than a year—overthinking every little detail until it became too much. Either I choose to stay in my rut or take the risk." Smiling at him encouragingly, I walk over to place a gentle hand on his forearm, squeezing the firm muscle beneath. "I think it's turned out alright so far, don't you think?"

Peter cups my hand and brings it to his cheek before feathering a soft kiss over the palm. I blush at the tender gesture and remember our kiss the other day—thoughts of other types of risk running through my head.

"Yeah, I do." His deep voice steals over my nerves, heightening my awareness of him until he loosens his grip, and we continue our survey of the shop. "Why do you say you were in a rut back then? What was happening?"

"Nothing." I laugh bitterly as sad memories flood me with loneliness. "I worked. I came home. Repeat. Similar to what you mentioned the other day, actually. It was a small town without much of a social scene—not that it would've helped me much. Generally, I'm a fairly shy person, more introverted, which makes it difficult to make friends."

"And you thought moving would change that?"

"I thought having more opportunities to try to change would be helpful. Or maybe I could ride the confidence high of moving by myself to meet new people." My lips twist in satisfaction. "And it worked. Despite my anxiety, I accepted your offer of lessons, didn't I? I'm doing the damn thing."

An image of the quote from an old Bachelorette promo flashes in my mind, but it's true, I realize. As I'm trying to reassure Peter, I'm reminding myself of how far I've come and what I've accomplished. Even our kiss would've seemed impossible a few months ago.

"Guess that means we should get started." A boyish grin brightens his face before handing me a pair of safety glasses. "Put these on for protection. I know I mentioned building a birdhouse, but why don't you help me with a small project first?"

Nervous energy rockets under my skin, making me feel jittery. The anxiety I mentioned perks up; I don't want to ruin his work or embarrass myself.

*Relax, he knows you're a beginner.*

Sliding the clear plastic glasses over my ears, a slight haze blurs my vision. High school days spent in science labs come back to me at the familiar experience.

"What's the project?" I watch as Peter sets a couple wood boards on the worktable.

"You're going to help me turn these pine boards into chair legs." He motions me closer and begins to show me how he measures and marks the wood for cutting. Handing over the ruler and pencil, he says, "Give it a try. I realize you know how to use a ruler already, but it's still worth being part of the process."

We work companionably for a half hour when Peter grabs a red tool with handles on either side of a center blade. He sets the tool in front of me. "This is a spokeshave. Have you ever seen one before?"

I shake my head no, and he explains, "It's going to help us curve the pine into the right shape for me to carve in the twisted rope detail. Ready to try?"

"Ready as I'll ever be." Taking the tool from him, I face the newly-cut leg when Peter moves to stand behind me—the intimate move raising the hair on the back of my neck in attention.

Hot breath tickles my ear as he whispers, "Don't worry. I'll be right here guiding you. You'll do fine."

Large hands cover mine to gently push forward, showing me the correct form. My gaze shifts to the intriguing display of his forearm muscles flexing.

I should focus on what I'm doing before I cut myself or send the spokeshave skittering to the floor, but Peter's warmth at my back is distracting. The earthy smell of sawdust mixed with his clean body wash surrounds me—a tantalizing scent urging me to breathe deeper. Unconsciously, I push back which causes something hard to nudge against my ass.

My lungs stutter as I realize he's getting aroused by our positions, too, and relief that I'm not the only one makes me daring. Arching my hips, I rub a little harder, and our hands stall on the spokeshave, its original purpose all but forgotten.

"Trying to tease me, sweetheart?" Peter slowly spurs me forward until I'm trapped between him and the table—the hard edge digging into my soft belly. Light fingertips drift over my neck as he brushes my hair over one shoulder; a featherlight kiss skims over the exposed skin, and I shiver in response.

Maybe I was trying to tease him. I didn't have a lot of experience with men, but things felt easy with Peter. For some reason, my usual fear refused to put up much of a fight when it came to him. And instead of questioning any deeper meaning, I'm going to roll with and see where it takes me.

"What are you going to do if I am?" The sultry voice isn't recognizable to my ears, but I guess the seductress inside me had never had a reason to appear before now.

"If my girl wants to play, who am I to refuse her?"

*His girl?* The possessive endearment makes my thighs clench in anticipation of his claiming. *God, listen to me. Claiming.* Like I'm living in some kind of fated mates novel.

Peter skirts a hand around my waist to glide under my shirt. "Is this alright?"

"Yes..." And immediately his hand continues its path upward until he cups one of my breasts, thumb flicking over the hardened tip.

"You know, I've never had someone out here before—never asked a woman home, let alone into my shop." Another hand lowers to the button of my jeans as he keeps playing with my nipple. "You wet, baby? Want me to lay you bare and let you soak this table with your cream as I eat this pussy?"

Somehow, he's managed to unzip my jeans and slip a hand down my panties without my notice until I feel rough fingertips probe my entrance. I moan at the contact, eager for him to reach a little higher and circle my clit.

"Mmm...that's exactly what you want. You need my tongue, baby?"

I nod frantically, and Peter whips me around so we're chest to chest. Removing the safety glasses we're both wearing, I stifle a laugh at how ridiculous we must've looked then any thoughts outside of Peter fly out the window as his mouth devours mine in a harsh kiss.

Wet, sucking sounds fill the room when he starts pumping his fingers deep—the palm of his hand slapping against the bundle of nerves aching for attention. "Please..." I beg, needing more—his hand, his tongue—I want everything.

Peter jerks away and rips off his plaid overshirt, leaving a plain white tee that molds to his chest. I grasp the hem of the shirt thinking to help him undress when he shakes his head. "Not yet, sweetheart. I just need this to protect you from any stray splinters. The tabletop's worn smooth, but I'd rather be safe than sorry."

Spreading the thick fabric over the table, he captures my hips in a firm grip and lifts me to settle on the hard surface. My nails dig into his shoulders for balance while admiration blooms in my chest. I'm not a light burden—extra curves abound—yet he picked me up like it was nothing, and my desire intensifies at the impressive feat.

"You weren't kidding...We're really going to do this." It's a statement more than a question because I'm not planning on changing my mind, but we're moving so fast I can't help a frisson of disbelief.

"If you're up for it." Peter's concerned gaze meets mine—a sweet tenderness that melts my previously guarded heart. Is it any wonder he bypassed all of my defenses?

Caressing his bearded cheek, I draw closer and trail kisses over the scratchy skin before landing on his lips. "Trust me, I want this—want *you*."

"Thank fuck." He presses another savage kiss to my mouth then urges me back. "Lie down, baby, and let's get these off." I feel a tug on my jeans and brace myself on shaky elbows as Peter peels them away along with my underwear.

The aluminum ceiling above reflects the sunlight filtering in from the open garage, and I notice prisms of color floating in the air. It almost feels like a dream when Peter's head dips, and the first brush of his lips against my inner thigh makes me jump.

"Easy, sweetheart," he murmurs, inching nearer to my core. With the first swipe of his tongue through my folds, I expel the breath I'd been holding and close my eyes—lifting my hips higher for his touch.

A desperate plea resounds in my head.

*More. Give me more.*

# CHAPTER SIX

## *PETER*

Anna trembles beneath me, and I fight to maintain control. Her heady taste coats my tongue—inciting a ravenous hunger to drink her down, savoring every sweet drop.

I'll never be able to look at this table the same or walk into my shop without remembering this moment. Pleasuring my girl, nibbling her clit, plunging my tongue deep—over and over again.

Sexy little mewls tumble from her, making the bulge behind my zipper try harder to get out. *Not yet, buddy. Not until I make her come.*

Whirling my tongue over her clit, I crisscross my middle and pointer finger to form a corkscrew and bury it in her pussy—eliciting a sharp inhale.

"Peter... Please..." Anna's nails scratch against my scalp as she holds my head down, and a brief chuckle bubbles up at her enthusiasm.

"Don't worry, baby. I'll take care of you." I keep pumping in and out with a twisting motion, making sure to rub against her g-spot until her pussy tightens around me—her back bending and thighs clenching around me at the orgasm.

My hand slows but doesn't stop—prolonging her pleasure—as I kiss her curvy body, skimming over her round stomach and generous breasts. The fact that I skipped exploring those particular delights bothers me, but given another chance, I'll make it up to her. I love how soft she is and wish I could stay enveloped by her forever.

Baby-fine curls cling to the sweat on her forehead and her brown eyes are cloudy with satisfaction. Pride swells in my chest as I drop quick pecks from her forehead down her nose before hovering over her mouth.

"Are you happy with where your teasing got you?"

Anna struggles to sit up until I help steady her, enfolding her pliant body in my arms. "I certainly got more than I bargained for but can't say I regret it."

"That's good to hear." Her admission alleviates some of my fear of moving too fast.

"But this particular lesson seems to have reached its conclusion. Maybe we can go inside and clean up?" She combs out several dust remnants clinging to her hair, and I agree with her suggestion. Once I ease her to the ground, Anna gets dressed, pulling her discarded jeans back on. "I have an odd habit of needing to shower whenever I visit you; I'm not sure what to think of it."

She teases me with a smile—its brightness punching me in the gut. "Don't blame me. You've instigated each event." I enclose her hand in mine as we head inside my cabin—deja vu hitting me when we arrive in my bathroom again.

"Fair point." Turning to face me, Anna bites her lip before lowering a hand to my stomach causing my muscles to clench at the contact. "What if we switched things up a bit?"

I tilt my head in consideration and ask, "What do you mean?"

She exhales a heavy breath and gestures towards the large walk-in shower in the corner. "Do you want to join me?"

Blood leaves my head so fast dizziness sets in. Surely, I didn't hear her correctly. "Can you repeat that?"

Doubt colors her expression as she tentatively asks again—fear infusing her voice. The sound brings all my protective instincts to the forefront, and I hurry to reassure her. "I would love nothing more than to get you bare beneath my hands, baby."

Grabbing the hem of my tee, I tear it over my head, waiting for her response. Anna's brown eyes trace down my chest before crawling back to meet my amused gaze. "Is it okay if I say I feel the same way?"

"Hell, yeah! And there's more to come; trust me."

Together we shuck our clothing in record time and stumble into the shower where I adjust the knobs until warm water splashes over us. Steam begins fogging the glass partition, and I grab a bottle of shampoo. Slowly, our hands run over slick skin as we take turns lathering soap on the other, washing away all traces of dust from the workshop.

Anna rises on her tiptoes to smooth a kiss over my lips and whispers, "I'm going to try something; if you don't like it, let me know."

"Babe, do anything you want. I'm yours." A strong declaration for such a short period of friendship, but I'm tired of holding back. Years have gone by, life passing me in a blur of loneliness. If Anna's willing, I want her in my life for good—not for a set number of lessons.

"You mean it, don't you?"

An inelegant snort punctures the heavy air, and I admit, "So much it might overwhelm you to the point of running for the hills."

She emits a low hum of disagreement. "Don't be so sure..." Her mouth travels from my lips to my neck then further south until she rests on her knees, innocent eyes peering up at me.

"Remember what I said about not liking this," she warns before wrapping a hand around my erection and bringing the mushroom head to her mouth.

The humid air clogs in my lungs as I watch her graze the tip with an experimental stroke. If she'd never been kissed before, then I know she sure as hell has never sucked a cock. That she wants to suck mine ensures my devotion forever.

More than the physical act itself, I know she's shedding her protective shell, prepared to put herself in such a vulnerable position for my benefit. And that trust weighs precious in my hands—I won't abuse it.

She laps at my dick in short licks, culminating in continuous spurts of pre-cum leaking downward. Shifting back, heat engulfs me as Anna's lips surround the tip, and an obscene slurping sound bounces off the walls.

"Fuck, baby! Just like that..." My hand grasps the back of her neck, but I resist forcing her further. Water stings my eyes as I continue to watch. She's too damn pretty on her knees for me; a bite of pain isn't going to cause me to miss a second.

Her throat works to swallow, and the undulation sends a shudder down my spine. Time is not on my side—an orgasm threatens to end the moment too soon. I need to wait, allow her to explore for as long as she wants.

*Because that's such a hardship—letting your girl continue to suck you off.*

# CHAPTER SEVEN

*ANNA*

Peter's taste fills my mouth, and it's unexpectedly delicious. My palm squeezes the base of his shaft—an answering jet of pre-cum hitting my throat—and I revel in the power I have over him. At first, paranoid thoughts of gagging or hating going down on him plastered themselves all over my mind, but I forced my attention on Peter's support and realized it was worth trying even if I failed to please him.

And his claim to be mine? It made me want to prove I'm a worthy partner. Now, those doubts spiral down the drain with the rest of the shower water. Rubbing my tongue on the sensitive ridge underneath, Peter jerks and lets loose another expletive. I may not be experienced, but it's easy enough to tell he enjoys my ministrations which goes a long way towards reassuring me.

"Anna... I'm so close..." The promise of his impending orgasm ignites my fervor, and I strain to take more of him. Seconds later, hot streams of cum surge from him and overflows between us as I struggle to swallow every last drop. When it finally stops, I release him with a pop and stand on unsteady legs.

"Guess you liked it, huh?" I tease while massaging his relaxed shoulder. His chest rises and falls with quick breaths, and I can't help but admire my handiwork.

*I did this to him.*

His answer is to capture a nipple between his lips, sucking hard before switching sides and releasing me. "Did you like that?"

*God, yes.*

"Now, brace your hands against the wall." He growls and whips me to face the wet tile. The abrupt change sends my head spinning, but I'm game for whatever he's planning. Teeth nipping my shoulder, Peter covers my splayed hands with his.

"I'm going to fuck you just like this. It's going to be deep and hard." The explicit words burn over my skin as eagerness settles between my thighs. "I know you're a virgin, so if you need me to be gentle, we'll wait because I don't have the restraint in me after having your lips wrapped around my dick."

"No, I need you now. I'm not so innocent that I've never used a vibrator before; I should be able to take you like this."

*I hope.*

"You've been playing alone with this pussy all these years, baby? Don't worry; that won't be necessary any longer." His hand slides over my stomach to part my curls before pinching my clit. The shocking move sends my body bolting into his, only to be slammed back to the tile—my breasts smashed against the flat surface.

"It's my turn now. Understand?" The heavy weight of his firm body traps me against the wall, removing any option for me to shift away.

*Not that I want to.*

Somehow, he's tapped into a dark fantasy of mine—to be dominated—and a whimper of need bubbles over. His feet nudge mine further apart as he uses one hand to guide himself to my pussy. My inner walls contract, needing his hard cock to tunnel inside.

"Ready, Anna?"

I barely get a confirmation out when Peter thrusts deep, and I gasp at the penetration. *Holy hell, he's thick.* Thicker than I'm used to—the strong rhythm he sets surpassing anything I've ever used at home.

My mind wanders in a dreamy haze as the pleasure builds inside my body, centering where Peter slams into me and blooming outward. It's difficult to believe I started the day a virgin, hoping something would grow between me and Peter; now I'm bent over in his shower as he takes me from behind.

But it doesn't feel wrong or dirty. A sense of belonging burrows into my heart overshadowing any negative judgement of my actions.

Suddenly, Peter shifts the angle of his thrusts, and thinking becomes impossible. "Please, Peter... Don't stop..."

His mouth nuzzles my neck and fingers circle my clit as his speed increases. "Come for me, sweetheart. Let me feel your pussy—"

My cry of release interrupts the explicit command, and Peter follows with a jerky slam of his hips that shoots warmth down my thighs as he pulls out. And a random thought of pregnancy flits about before disappearing.

Reaching for the shower knobs, he turns off the cold water, and our labored breathing echoes around the stall. I pivot around and drop my forehead to Peter's chest—exhausted but content.

"If we can manage, it might be a good idea to go somewhere where we can't accidentally slip and break our necks." I laugh and agree with his assessment. With the weakness still radiating in my legs, falling in the slick shower doesn't seem so far-fetched.

"And we can dry off; the soggy prune life ain't for me."

He shrugs and hands me a towel. "I don't know. You still look sexy as fuck to me."

Apparently, our lovemaking hasn't robbed me of the ability to blush because heat sparks at the compliment. Dipping my head in sudden shyness, I pat away the drops of water clinging to my skin, focusing on the simple task instead of responding—and reality seeps into the silence.

But it's not tinged with fear or regret; instead, a sense of optimism reigns supreme. All this time I've worried so much about embarrassing myself or saying the wrong thing around people that I've avoided even the possibility by shutting myself away. Yet, here I am after making the decision to try something new—to trust Peter—and things haven't exploded in my face.

Whatever happens next, I've proven risks are worth the potential rewards.

An overwhelming need to share the revelation with Peter explodes in a rush of words. "You're the only man to ever say such a thing to me, and I don't know if it's post-orgasmic hormones or your *teaching* skills." He grins at that last part. "But I really like you. You claimed to be mine, but I won't hold you to promises made in the heat of the moment if this is just a fling for you."

Buzzing drones in my ear while blood rushes to my head at the uncharacteristic outburst. My hands clench in the terry cloth surrounding me as I wait for his answer.

*Please, don't let me regret this.*

# CHAPTER EIGHT

### PETER

"You done?" I knot the towel around my waist and enfold her into my arms as she nods. Vulnerability veils her brown eyes, and tenderness softens my own gaze. "Good. To your points: this is not a fling, and I meant what I said."

Swaying closer, a brilliant smile transforms her face. "Glad to hear we're on the same page... Though, I feel like I shouldn't be this content with how long we've known each other."

"The good news is we don't need to follow anyone else's timeline. If we're happy, that's all that matters." I drop a brief kiss on the tip of her nose. "And I, for one, am extremely fucking happy."

More than I thought possible.

"Alright. Yes. Me, too." She stutters staccato sentences before chuckling. "Sorry...we just had this serious DTR conversation, and my mind's kind of reeling."

"DTR?" I wrack my brain for what the acronym stands for as I lead her to the bedroom, and we sit on the edge of the bed.

"Define the relationship. Don't worry, I didn't know what it meant before I joined a dating relationship group."

"You're going to explain that to me later, but for now, why don't we discuss our terms." Going all in, what I really want from her spills out. "Marriage. A family."

"Not all today, I hope." She bumps my shoulder playfully. "But I can get on board with that future. If you haven't noticed, I'm all about rolling with whatever comes my way these days."

"Have I mentioned how glad I am that you've made that decision. I know it hasn't been easy for you." Anna's commitment to changing her life inspires me and allows my own dreams to be voiced—to possibly be realized.

One was already coming true by finding a woman like Anna. Sweet, curvy, and smart, and she just fell into my lap by chance.

*Thank god she did.*

"You made it easier. In a way, you're kind of my reward," she whispers, reaching for my hand and kissing the back of it.

"Funny; I'd say it was the other way around." Lowering my head, our mouths meet in a gentle kiss as we fall back to the mattress. No more words were needed, just me loving my woman.

# EPILOGUE ONE

The high-pitched squeal of a table saw pierces my ears as I find Peter hunched over his latest project. Pausing before he notices my arrival, I take the time to admire my husband.

A long-sleeve woolen shirt rolled up to his elbows reveals tan forearms that lead to capable hands. Hands that have touched every part of me yet still maintain enough power to shoot a shiver down my spine at the thought of him touching me again.

Gratitude threatens to burst from my chest as I'm overwhelmed with how lucky I've been to find a man like Peter. Dedicated and kind, I never doubt his love—despite our whirlwind beginning. At least, it seemed that way for me; he was ready to marry me the same day we made love the first time. But we waited for six months before I finally gave in and trusted what we had as the real deal.

The sawing stops and quiet settles over the room—broken only by the chirping birds outside, enjoying the miniature bird resort we've made with all the houses I've added. Tilting his safety glasses to rest on top of his head, Peter smiles. "You need something, baby?"

"Everything's good to go with the website, but I want your opinion before it goes live."

A year ago, he'd finally suggested becoming partners with Cora and Chris, but they'd turned him down. They appreciated his work and wanted to keep him as an employee but weren't looking to share a portion of their business. That had been a rough couple of months as he continued to work for them even though his dream had been shattered.

"Whatever you think's best is good enough for me; I trust you." Peter circles my waist and drops a kiss on the side of my neck, nibbling his way to my ear. I know where this is leading, but I can't be distracted—other tasks are on the agenda for today.

Leaning back, I force a disapproving frown. "None of that until you take a look. It's the official gateway for online orders; I want you to have a say."

Once Peter had recovered from the blow to his future dream, he rallied and worked harder than ever to get his craftsman business off the ground. Long hours spent at Cora and Chris's making custom but generic furniture followed by evenings in his shop creating one-of-a-kind pieces dominated his days for months. Until we reached today—the day we launch online to garner a whole new side of business. Local word-of-mouth has been keeping us afloat, but we're dreaming bigger now.

He sighs, grabs my hand, and starts walking us back to the cabin. "One quick run-through, then I want you on your back in our bed. I haven't fucked my wife in forever."

My eyes roll at the dramatization even as a flurry of arousal seeps to my core. "Try a few hours. If I recall correctly, you woke me in the most delightful way."

"Like I said: forever ago." He winks with the teasing remark, and we head towards our combined office at the back of the home. Peter's appetite for me never wanes, and it goes a long way towards shoring up the firm foundation of trust and love I have for him.

I never thought someone like him—or anyone—would ever need me, love me like he does. And it definitely never occurred to me that I could meet the love of my life on a routine errand that catalyzed the domino effect of our relationship.

Yet, here we are, and I couldn't be happier.

I thought I needed an entire community of people surrounding me to feel fulfilled, and while we have a few great friends, all I ever really needed was him.

One man to love and support me forever.

# EPILOGUE TWO

*PETER*
THREE YEARS LATER

"What are you doing out here?" I sneak behind Anna as she tries to hide something under a cloth sheet. For weeks now, I've known something's up because tools would be shifted when I arrived at the shop most mornings, but I attributed it to bad memory. Now, I see I wasn't going crazy—someone had been using things without my knowledge, and I've found the culprit: my wife.

"You should be resting," I scold, my hand cupping her pregnant stomach. The fact that she's carrying our baby still stuns me at times. We've worked hard to get my business up and running, leaving no time for children, but after years of hard work, we'd agreed it was time to try. Now, a baby's on the way, and I couldn't be happier.

"I'm fine." She waves my concern away. "Why don't you go back to the house, and I'll be right behind you." Anna tries escaping my grasp, but I stop her retreat with a hand on her hip.

"Not until I know what you're up to. Come on; show me." I motion to whatever she's hiding, and a mulish expression transforms her usually smiling face.

"It's supposed to be a surprise."

"Trust me, I'm *surprised* to find my pregnant wife padding around my workshop unsupervised." Anything could happen to her out here, and while I'd usually trust her to be safe, I'm not taking any risks with her or the baby. This pregnancy has amped up all the possessive caveman tendencies I thought I'd learned to control after tying Anna to me with a ring and a promise.

"I'm not doing anything dangerous; I'll be fine. Now, go back to the house." She injects a firm note to her voice that I imagine her using with our son when he's born, and it gets me even more worked up. My cock swells at the challenge, needing to dominate her willfulness.

Skimming my lips over her ear, I warn, "Don't think I can't get it out of you. I'll sit your ass on this table like that first time—only I'll lick your pretty pussy to the very edge of a climax, holding back what you need until you give me what I want."

"I'm not sure that's much of a punishment...You're incapable of letting me suffer for too long, aren't you?"

Damn, she's right, but I'd try like hell to last as long as I could. "Are you refusing my request?"

Anna stays silent for a moment before releasing an exasperated breath. "No, I'll show you, but it's not finished yet." She brandishes a small wooden heart, jagged edges running along the sides. "This was going to be an anniversary gift with our initials carved into it, but I'm struggling to get the heart-shape right."

Warmth rises in my chest, my heart beating double-time. She made me a gift—a heart—it was fucking adorable. Over the years, we've continued our lessons in the shop, some more educational than others if we managed to keep our hands off each other. And she impressed me with how quickly she picked things up.

"This looks good to me, baby. Thank you." I brush a gentle kiss over her lips before taking the heart and setting it aside. Guiding her back, I ask, "You've been working hard, haven't you?"

"Maybe I deserve a reward instead of punishment, hmm?"

Chuckling, I rub a hand over her ass and squeeze the plump flesh, happy to reenact that afternoon I tasted her for the first time. "Whatever my girl wants."

*Always.*

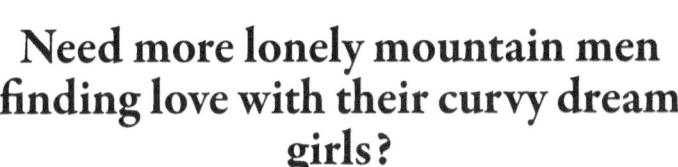

# Need more lonely mountain men finding love with their curvy dream girls?

Check out the Lumberjacks of High Ridge series!

## Kept by the Beast

*All Poppy wanted was a relaxing trip to the cute mountain town of High Ridge. She didn't plan on getting stranded with no one to call for help. What's a shy, curvy girl to do?*

*Asa is known as the town's Beast. Large and foreboding, women run in fear and revulsion. But when this mountain man happens upon a curvy damsel in distress, could she be the one woman to accept him for who he is?*

*Two virgins stranded in a cabin...Things are heating up on the mountain when a curvy girl meets this beastly lumberjack in a steamy story of insta-love!*

# THANKS FOR READING & DON'T FORGET TO RATE/ REVIEW!

Please consider leaving a rating/review on Amazon, Goodreads, Instagram, TikTok, and/or any other sites you review on.
Ratings & reviews are the #1 way to support an indie author like me.
They don't have to be long or even positive (though I hope you enjoyed this book!). All the algorithms care about are QUANTITY.
The more reviews, the more my books are shown to other potential readers!
And they serve as guides to readers on whether or not to take a chance on an indie author.
Also, don't miss out on free books and up-to-date release information. You can sign up for my newsletter here.
I appreciate your support!
**XO, Hallie**

# ABOUT THE AUTHOR

Hallie prefers steamy, insta-love stories where curvy girls are claimed by filthy-talking heroes. And when she ran out of reading material, she decided to write her own stories. If you want a quick, hot read, she's your girl!